Making Millions

ERIKA MCGANN lives in Dublin in her own secret clubhouse (which is actually an apartment) and spends her time solving mysteries and having brilliant adventures (well, she writes about them anyway). She likes cold weather (because it's an excuse to drink hot chocolate by the gallon) and cheesy jokes (because cheesy jokes are always funny, even when they're not funny). Her first book about Cass and the Bubble Street Gang, *The Clubhouse Mystery*, is also published by The O'Brien Press.

Making Millions

Erika McGann

illustrated by Vince Reid

THE O'BRIEN PRESS
DUBLIN

Leabharlanna Poiblí Chathair Baile Átha Cliath

Dublin City Public Libraries

First published 2017 by
The O'Brien Press Ltd,
12 Terenure Road East, Rathgar,
Dublin 6, D06 HD27 Ireland.
Tel: +353 1 4923333; Fax: +353 1 4922777
E-mail: books@obrien.ie.
Website: www.obrien.ie

ISBN: 978-1-84717-921-0

1 3 5 7 8 6 4 2
17 19 21 20 18

Cover and internal illustrations by Vince Reid.
Printed and bound by Norhaven Paperback A/S, Denmark.

The paper in this book is produced using pulp from managed forests.

Published in

DUBLIN
UNESCO
City of Literature

For Milo and Esben

Acknowledgements

Thanks to Vince Reid for more brilliant and hilarious illustrations – I looked forward to seeing every new one – and to Emma Byrne, who puts it all together and makes the book look wonderful. Thanks to Ruth Heneghan, Geraldine Feehily and everyone at The O'Brien Press for all their enthusiasm for the series. And a big thanks to my editor, Helen Carr, for being so patient and lovely to work with.

Chapter One

Have you got a brilliant brain? Sounds like a great thing, right? And it is, for the most part. But having a brilliant brain is no walk in the park. I should know. *I've* got a brilliant brain, and sometimes it's *exhausting*.

In case we haven't met before, my name is Cass. I'm smart and funny and ten years old. I'm also a genius detective. That's where the brilliant brain comes in.

When solving mysteries with my two best friends – Lex and Nicholas – my brilliant brain is invaluable. We had a whopper of a mystery recently. Someone was breaking into our secret clubhouse (that's right, we've got a secret clubhouse. It's got walls and a door and everything, and it's in a very secret location, in the hedge at the end of Mr McCall's field. But keep that to yourself – it's a secret).

After lots of detecting and spying, and dangerous adventures involving bulls and dogs and screeching cats, we finally figured out that it was Lex's granny and her card-playing friends who were breaking in. We built them their own clubhouse (to keep them happy and out of *ours*), but that's not important right now. What's important is that as soon as the mystery was solved my brain got bored. It started to itch. It was *itching* for another exciting mystery to solve. And that's the exhausting thing about having a brilliant brain. The *itch*.

So I was on the lookout for the Bubble Street Gang's next great adventure (that's the name of our secret club, by the way … *shhh*). And I found it. Want to hear what it is? Are you sure? 'Cos it'll blow your mind. Here goes …

There's an invisible boy in my class.

A real one. I don't mean a boy that everyone ignores and it's like he's invisible. I mean an actual, real-life, totally see-through boy who's actually, completely invisible.

I know what you're thinking. How do I know there's an invisible boy in my class if he's invisible? Well, sit back and let me tell you how a genius detective works. You see, I saw his name in the register on the teacher's desk (my teacher, Mr Freebs, was giving me a lecture on how important it is to *get along* with everyone, even people you don't like, even people like snobby Nathan Wall, even evil snobby snobs like *Nathan Wall*. I'm getting off the point here – basically, I was standing at the teacher's desk and I was too embarrassed to look him in the eye, so I was staring down at the desk. On the desk was the class register. In the register was the name of a new boy).

Martyn Nowak is the invisible boy's name. He's new to our class and I think the school is trying to hide the fact that he exists because, on the first day of term, Mr Freebs didn't make him stand up so we could all say 'hello' to him. That's what usually happens when there's a new kid in class; they have to stand up and tell everybody their name and where they're from, and then we all say, 'Hello, Martyn' (or whatever their name is) together. Then the new kid gets all embarrassed and sits down.

Mr Freebs *loves* that sort of stuff, and there's no way he'd leave out the embarrassing introductions unless he was under strict orders from the school.

I know what you're thinking now; it's what I thought at first. Maybe the new boy just wasn't in that day. Maybe he was sick.

Maybe he was. But he didn't show up the next day either. Or the day after that, or the day after that, or the day after that. Weeks have gone by and Martyn Nowak has never appeared. The new boy has *never* shown up for school.

At least that's what an ordinary person might think. But I know better. I know he *is* there; in the front row on the very left, in the seat that looks empty, but isn't.

'It's just an empty seat, Cass.'

That's my best friend, Nicholas. He doesn't believe me about the invisible boy. We argued about it one time, during little break.

'People can't go invisible,' he said, 'it's impossible. Except for maybe ... maybe there's a special suit somewhere designed by scientists, covered in mirrors and things, that can make someone *look* like they're invisible. But even if there is such a suit, there's no way a boy in our class has one.'

Nicholas got this far-off look in his eye and I knew he was wishing he could make that suit. He is quite good at making costumes and things, it's kind of his gift. And it's lucky he is good at making things because when it comes to investigating the paranormal – ghosts and monsters and invisible boys – Nicholas has no talent whatsoever.

'If there's no invisible boy,' I said, 'then who is the new kid in the class register?'

'Why don't you just ask Mr Freebs?'

'Because I think Mr Freebs is under orders to keep it a secret,' I replied.

Nicholas rolled his eyes. 'Come on, that's just silly.'

'Oh yeah?' I said. 'Then how come when I tested him, he *failed*. The other day I said, "Mr Freebs, I think Martyn left his book on my table", and Mr Freebs said, "Who?" and got all flustered. Then he started messing with some papers on his desk and told me to go outside and play 'cos it was lunchtime. If he's not hiding something, why didn't he just tell me about Martyn? Why did he act all suspicious?'

'I don't know,' said Nicholas, 'maybe ... maybe he was just flustered that day and–'

'And maybe there's an invisible boy in our class.'

Nicholas shook his head and rolled his eyes again.

'Fine,' I said, 'I'll prove it.'

'How?'

'I don't know yet, but I will.'

Nicholas snorted. 'Yeah, right.'

'What's got into you?!'

'What do you mean?'

'You've been huffy all day,' I said.

'No I haven't. I'm fine.'

'You're in a bad mood. Why?'

'I'm not in a bad mood, Cass, just leave me alone!'

'Are you sure you're all right?'

That's my other best friend, Lex. She's good at being in the middle when me and Nicholas have little arguments like this. I shut up for a bit and Nicholas finally said,

'My mum won't let me go to the costume masterclass that's on in the arts centre next month.'

'How come?' said Lex.

'She says it's too expensive. Even dad says it's too dear.'

'Don't you already do an art class every

week?' I said.

'That's different,' said Nicholas, 'that's general art stuff. This is a costume masterclass. That means it's not just for anyone – it's for people who are already good at making costumes and want to get even better. I'm a *good* costume designer, but I want to be a master costume designer. So I need to do a *masterclass.*'

'Yeah, but if you quit your regular art classes then there'd be money for the masterclass, right?'

Nicholas frowned. 'I can't quit my art classes, they're essential for my artistic development.'

That sounded a bit silly, but I didn't say so. 'Then what about your acting classes?'

'Quit my acting classes?' Nicholas looked

like I'd just shoved a load of ice cubes down his shirt. 'I can't quit my acting classes, they're essential!'

'What about the other one?' Lex asked. 'The voice classes? Do you really need them?'

Now it looked like the ice cubes had slid down the back of Nicholas's pants making him jump off his seat.

'My voice classes?' he said. 'No, no, no, no, you don't understand. How can I become a great actor if I don't know how to use my voice properly? Those classes are *essential*.'

I was starting to think that Nicholas didn't understand the meaning of the word essential.

(New) definition of essential: not important at all. Not at all. Not even a tiny teeny little bit.

'Well,' I said, running out of patience, 'then I guess you can't do the extra special masterclass thing. Too bad.'

Nicholas went all huffy again and didn't speak to me for the rest of the break. But that was okay, because I had a mystery to solve. How do you prove there's an invisible boy in your classroom if you can't point him out?

It felt a bit weird to be doing this investigation all by myself. I usually work with a team – that's why we started the Bubble Street Gang in the first place – but for this one, I was going it alone.

So I took out a very special notebook that I'd been saving for a very special case. I got it for my birthday – it has 'TOP SECRET' stamped on the front cover and at the top of each page. I opened the notebook, picked up a pen and started planning my very first solo investigation:

Operation Invisible Boy

My ideas for exposing Invisible Boy were pure genius. First, I left my eraser on his desk, right in front of his chair. If the eraser moved during class then that would prove there was somebody sitting there. The eraser did not move. Hmm, turns out Invisible Boy is clever. But that's no problem. I'm cleverer.

Next, during music time when we're allowed get musical instruments from the box under the window, I snuck up behind Invisible Boy with a pair of cymbals and banged them together really loudly to make him jump and scream. There was no scream. Invisible Boy is made of stern stuff. But that's okay. So am I.

Then, during art class, I hit on the perfect plan. I took a little pot of blue paint and a paintbrush from the art drawer, and I snuck up behind Invisible Boy's chair. It wouldn't take much, just a few tiny, barely-even-there drops. You see, even if Invisible Boy is invisible, he's still *there*. There's still a boy sitting in that chair. And if someone accidentally spilled a few drops of paint on the back of his jumper (don't worry, it's water-soluble paint so it'll wash off), you'd see that the paint has landed on *something*, even if you couldn't see the something.

I crept up behind the chair, dipping just the very tip of the paintbrush in the pot of blue paint and then, ever so carefully, flicked the paintbrush towards the chair. BIG mistake.

It was more than a few teeny, tiny drops. One blob of paint landed on Invisible Boy's desk (he must have leapt out of the way at the last second – he's so *sneaky*), and another blob of paint landed on Archie Quinn's cheek.

Archie Quinn sits in the chair next to Invisible Boy's and he's really funny. He told a joke in class once that made me laugh so hard my sides hurt for ages. There was a time when I thought me and Archie could be good friends, but then he glared at me with that splash of blue paint on his face and now I think that time has passed.

'Cass Okara,' Mr Freebs cried from across

the room, 'what on *earth* do you think you're doing?'

I don't usually get so embarrassed that I wish the ground would swallow me up, but I did then.

'Sorry, Mr Freebs. Sorry, Archie.'

Chapter Two

Because of the awful blue paint incident I was not allowed out to the yard at lunch-time. Instead, I had to put away all the art stuff that was used during class. There was so much of it.

'All right there, Cass?' Mr Freebs said as he sat writing as his desk.

'Yes, Mr Freebs.'

'Good. Don't forget the glue on Carol's desk, will you?'

Carol hadn't even bothered to put the lid back on the glue. Some people are so lazy.

I suppose it was fair enough that I be punished for splatting Archie Quinn with paint

mostly-by-accident, so I decided I'd make the best of it and think of other things while I slaved away for the whole of lunchtime.

Since my solo investigation, Operation Invisible Boy, was not going very well, I decided it was about time the Bubble Street Gang had another real adventure together. Me, Lex and Nicholas started this secret club for a reason – to investigate mystery, solve crime, start small businesses and generally do exciting stuff – and recently we hadn't been doing any exciting stuff.

While watching the rest of the class leave to go outside and play (urgh, and I was *dying* for a good game of space invaders!), I had noticed that Nicholas was still looking down in the dumps. Why he would want to go to *another* outside-of-school class is beyond me, but like my granny always says, each to their own – which means, other people are weird and you've just got to live with it. Besides, Rule No. 10 of the Bubble Street Gang's clubhouse rules is as follows:

10. Any member can demand help from other members in matters of life or death (or if it's just really, really important).

This was not a matter of life or death, but it probably felt like it to Nicholas, so the gang would do its duty and help. But how?

How could we convince his parents to fork out more money? And was that even possible? I mean, parents have only got so much money, right? How can they give out more money than they've got?

Then it hit me like a bolt of lightning. *We'd* make the money to get Nicholas to his masterclass! The Bubble Street Gang was about to have its very first business adventure. We would set up a company, we would have invoices and paperwork and deadlines, we'd yell at people down phone lines and draw big graphs on the walls. And we'd make a pile of cash; we'd be rich, we'd be rolling in it, we'd be ...

'Millionaires!'

'Sorry, Cass?' Mr Freebs glanced up from his desk with a strange look on his face.

'Nothing, Mr Freebs,' I said, pushing the art drawer closed.

I was smiling. I couldn't help it. The others were going to *love* this plan.

'But what *is* the plan?' Nicholas, as always, started with a question.

'To become millionaires,' I said.

'Yeah, but how?'

'We set up a company.'

'What kind of company?'

'A money-making one.'

'Yeah, but what will the company *do*?'

'Stop getting hung up on the details, Nicholas, it'll all get worked out.'

'By who?'

'Urgh! By me, okay? I'll sort it.'

This was not the madly excited reaction I'd been hoping for when I announced:

Operation Start a Company and Make Loads of Money for Nicholas's Masterclass and Probably Also Become Millionaires

That's not a very catchy mission title, I know. I'm going to work on that one.

At least Lex was excited about it.

'That sounds brilliant!' she said. 'We can use the laptop my gran got me for my birthday, and have our company meetings in the clubhouse. It'll be so much fun!'

That Saturday afternoon I headed to the clubhouse with my dad's old mobile (the screen was smashed and the phone wouldn't stay switched on for very long, but really it was just a prop. I wanted to make the right entrance). I walked down the lane by Mr McCall's field (there were two horses in it at the moment and neither of them were very friendly), turned right at the end and crossed the plank bridge over the stream to the clubhouse.

Our clubhouse is brilliant. No, it's better than brilliant, it's awesome! We built it ourselves, in a tree in the hedge at the end of Mr McCall's field, and it's the greatest thing we've ever done. No one knows it's there. Well, except for Lex's granny, but she won't tell. She's cool, like us.

I crept up to the door and I could hear Lex and Nicholas inside. Perfect. I put the phone to my ear, marched through the door and yelled, 'I don't care if the president's having a giant birthday party and he's bought up all the jellies in the country, I want twenty boxes delivered here by five o'clock tomorrow. Your finest jellies only. Raid the president's stash if you have to. Capiche?'

Definition of capiche (pronounced 'capeesh'): not really sure, but they say it a lot in old gangster films, usually after they've demanded something, and I think it makes me sound like a boss.

I slammed the phone down on the table like I was hanging up, even though it was a mobile and I should have just pressed the screen. Then I stood and smiled at Lex and Nicholas, waiting for a reaction.

'What was that?' said Nicholas.

'Oh, just me being the boss. That's how bosses order things. They don't ask, they just give orders.'

'Uh-huh.' He didn't look very impressed.

'Anyway,' I said, sitting down, 'I think I should be the CEO of our new company because I'm good at giving orders over the phone and things like that.'

'You can be the CEO,' Nicholas said, 'if you can tell me what CEO means.'

'It's means the boss.'

'Yeah, I know it means the boss, but what do the letters stand for?'

I only paused for a second. 'Chief of Everything ... in the Office.'

I wasn't entirely sure that was right, but I could tell Nicholas didn't know either because he just grumbled and said, 'Fine.'

'Can we start the meeting then?' said Lex.

She was sitting up very straight in front of the mini laptop her granny had given her. It's a second-hand one and the last owner put silvery princess stickers all over it (not really

Lex's thing), but it's purple underneath the silver stickers, which is quite cool.

'You guys can decide on all the company stuff,' she said, 'and I'll take the minutes of the meeting.'

'What?' I said. 'You're going to time us?'

'No, the *minutes*. That's what you call it when you take notes of what everybody says in a meeting. The minutes.'

'Oh. Okay then, will we start?'

'Go for it,' said Nicholas.

'Okay then, let's start. As CEO I hereby declare this meeting ... started.'

There was silence for a while.

'Well?' said Nicholas.

'Well what?' I said.

'Aren't you going to start?'

'Yeah, but ... what do we talk about?'

'About the company we're setting up. How we're going to make enough money for my masterclass.'

'Sure, okay.' I paused again. 'Anybody got any ideas?'

Nicholas sighed. 'I thought you would.'

'I do ... I will, but let's hear any other ones first. Lex, what do you think our company should do to make money?'

Lex went bright red. 'I'm just taking the minutes.'

'Hmm,' I said, 'all right then, I'll go. We could make something and sell it.'

'Okay,' said Nicholas, 'like what?'

I couldn't think of anything we could make that people would buy, so then I said,

'Or we could provide some service or something, like babysitting.'

'Who's going to let a bunch of ten-year-olds babysit their babies?' Nicholas said. 'We're too young for that.'

'Dog-walking!' I said. 'We're not too young for that. Anyone can walk a dog.'

'Bianca's got that covered, you know she has. She already walks every dog on the street.'

'So? We could be the rival company.'

'She's in big school, Cass. People won't trust us with their dogs when they can get a thirteen-year-old to do it. She's practically a grown-up.'

I frowned, but I knew he was right. Bianca owned the dog-walking market.

'Any other ideas?' I said.

There weren't any. We sat in silence for ages, ate some cookies, and went home.

Lex's minutes of our first ever company meeting were really, really short.

Chapter Three

'Dad, how do you become a millionaire?'

My dad smiled. 'If I knew that, Cass, we'd have a better car and I wouldn't have had to walk to work this morning.'

It was cold that morning and the car wouldn't start. I like our car; it's creaky and it has a funny smell (which isn't a *bad* smell, just a funny one), but it's also a bit moody. Sometimes it won't go when the weather's not right. I think it just doesn't like driving in the rain.

We were in an antique shop (that's a shop full of old furniture and other rubbish) and I was following my dad through a maze of old trunks and chairs and wardrobes. He loves that stuff. He'll buy a grubby old table and polish it up, then he'll sell it on or keep it or give it away as a present. Our house is full of old furniture.

'So you don't know how to become a millionaire?' I said.

'Why do you want to be a millionaire?'

''Cos it'd be brilliant. I could do whatever I wanted and go wherever I wanted, and I could buy *everything* I've ever wanted.'

Dad was opening and closing the doors on a cupboard, running his fingers over the hinges.

'Do you think you'd like that?' he said.

'Yes.'

'Getting whatever you wanted all the time? Wouldn't you get bored?'

I thought of a games room with an air hockey table and arcade machines, and an outdoor pool that I could do cannonballs into and float around on a giant lilo.

'Nope, definitely wouldn't get bored.'

'Hmm,' was all my dad said.

'Dad,' I asked, lifting up a tiny label that was tied to a mirror, 'what do the numbers on these little labels mean?'

'That's the price, honey.'

I nearly choked. 'Three hundred and fifty euro for a mirror? It's not even new!'

The woman behind the counter pursed her lips and looked down at me through narrowed eyes. I dropped the label.

'That mirror's Edwardian,' Dad said, moving on to an old writing desk, 'and in very good condition too. That's a fair price.'

'How can it cost so much when it's old?'

'People like old things, they've got character. And they've got history too. So they're
worth more.'

I looked around the dusty old shop that
smelled like the inside of a waterproof
jacket. I couldn't believe it. Half of the stuff
was cracked or chipped and looked like it
had been sitting in a junkyard for years.
One chest of drawers was even missing all its
drawers! And people bought this stuff?

It felt like a light bulb had literally pinged
to life right above my head: people will pay a
fortune for old, broken rubbish!

A plan for the Bubble Street Gang's first
company started forming in my mind. We'd
be millionaires by next week.

Operation Invisible Boy: Update

Very sure Invisible Boy kicked football at me in schoolyard (Nicholas said a gust of wind blew it, but that would have been one epic gust of wind). Kicked ball back really hard, hoping it would bounce off Invisible Boy and prove he was there. Did not bounce off Invisible Boy. Bounced off wall instead and then hit Jim Brick's little brother. Little brother Brick screamed really loud and then cried a lot. Lost another lunchtime to classroom-cleaning duty.

'What about this?' Nicholas held up a Transformer figure with one missing arm.

'Is it old?' I said.

'Got it for my seventh birthday.'

'Then stick it in the cardboard box.'

I was helping Nicholas go through his room to find stuff to sell in our Jumble Sale. That was the plan to make our first million. A Jumble Sale.

We were going to set up a table in my driveway and sell off everything of ours that was old and broken. I had heaps of stuff in my room – a whole storage box full – mostly thanks to the annoying baby twins (that is, my little sister and brother, Pippi and Ade). They're only two years old, but they cause more destruction than two full-grown Tyrannosaurus rexes. They're constantly breaking my stuff and, whenever they do, my parents say something like, 'Oh Cass, they just want to play with you,' and then dump whatever broken toy it is into the plastic box in my wardrobe. So all my poor, destroyed stuff is in one place. Nicholas's old and broken stuff was harder to find.

I was kneeling on his bed, trying to squeeze down the gap between the bed and the wall. There was something shiny down there in the dark. I squeezed down further, slipped and got stuck.

'Ah! Nick, help me!'

Nicholas grabbed me by the ankles and dragged me out of the bed-wall space.

'*Don't* call me Nick,' he snapped.

I brushed my hair out of my face and held

up a pair of round spectacles. 'Look what I found. Gold! And they're a bit skewy too. Perfect.'

'They're my Intelligent Character glasses. We're not selling those.'

Nicholas made a grab for the glasses, but I stood up on the bed and held them out of his way.

'Nice try, Nick,' I said, 'but you're standing in hot lava.'

'Don't call me Nick.'

He tried to pretend he was annoyed, but I'd seen the smile on his face as he looked down at his feet.

It's our favourite game for when we're stuck indoors: Hot Lava. The floor is hot lava, which will swallow you up and turn you to ash unless you keep to the safety of the rocks

(the 'rocks' in any room are the furniture; the bed, the chair, the desk, a cushion on the ground, etc.)

'I *need* those,' Nicholas said, still eyeing the spectacles in my hand, 'for when I'm playing a professor or a librarian ... or an evil scientist. Give them back.'

'Come get 'em.'

Nicholas jumped onto the bed, but I was too quick. I snatched a pillow and fired it across the floor, then I leapt across the river of burning lava. It was a wobbly landing but I made it to the pillow rock.

'That's cheating,' Nicholas said, 'you can't make new rocks.'

'You can make 'em if you can find 'em, Nicholas. Get your head in the game.'

I jumped to the chair in front of the desk.

It was one of those swivel ones and it spun around and around when I landed on it, making me dizzy. Nicholas dived onto a t-shirt that lay balled up on the floor.

'I'll get those glasses,' he growled at me.

'Oh yeah? Even though you're standing on a tiny rock and there's a lava tidal wave coming?'

Nicholas turned around and raised his arms over his face in horror (he's so good at the acting stuff, it makes it all feel very real).

'Oh no!' he cried, and leapt into the cardboard box with all the broken toys and pulled a woollen blanket over his head for protection.

I managed to stay ahead of him for the rest of the game and, by the time we were tired and out of breath, he was back on the bed and I was sitting on the desk. Just then the door opened and Lex came in carrying a black bin bag that looked too heavy for her.

'Lex, no!' me and Nicholas both cried out, reaching out our hands.

'Oh,' Lex said, looking down at the floor, 'am I in the lava?'

'You're in the lava,' I said.

'Never mind.' She walked into the middle of the room and emptied the bin bag onto the carpet. 'Check out all the broken stuff I found at home. Did you guys find anything?'

'These glasses,' I said, holding them up before Nicholas snatched them out of my hand.

'Do you really think people are going to want to buy this stuff, Cass?' said Lex.

'I wouldn't believe it either,' I said, 'if I hadn't watched my own dad pay actual money for a broken bookshelf. Trust me, this is going to work.'

Chapter Four

Every house on the street got one of our brilliant flyers, even a few houses on Mole Road until we ran out. It was going to be huge.

The table was set out at the end of my driveway and it was covered – COVERED – in interesting and valuable stuff. Mum had given me some sticky labels, so we cut them into little stickers and wrote the prices on them.

Minecraft action figure, not complete with sword or bow – €4.50

Baby doll that pees (but doesn't because she's full of play-dough) – €6.50

Transformers figure with missing arm – €3.00

Inline skates with only two wheels each – €9.50

Behind the rows and rows of broken toys we had the games. They were my idea after I saw a 'Guess How Many Sweets in the Jar' game at a fundraiser at my mum's work. We cleaned out a huge mayonnaise jar and filled it with jellies. I'd had to convince the other two about this one – it meant *all* of us spending *all* of our pocket money to buy enough jellies.

'You have to spend money to make money,' I said.

'That makes absolutely no sense,' said Nicholas.

I won out in the end and bought the sweets. I picked jellies because they're cheap and they look lovely and colourful in a jar, but now I was thinking they were a bad choice. Lex is a sucker for jellies.

'Did you open the jelly jar?' I asked as she straightened up the headless dolls in the middle of the table.

'No,' she said, but she was blushing.

'There were two reds on top, and now

there's not.'

There was a pause.

'I only had a couple,' she said.

'You *can't* eat the jellies, Lex. I counted them when I put them in, now I don't know how many there are. How many did you eat?'

'I don't know. A few?'

'Urgh.'

I opened the jar, tipped the jellies into an empty biscuit tin, counted them and put them back in. It took ages.

'No touching the jelly jar,' I said firmly.

'All right, I promise.'

'How's the hoop game going to work?' asked Nicholas.

I'd found this game in my storage box of broken stuff – it was a board with bulls-eyes on it and in the middle of each bulls-eye was a hook. You could hang the board on the wall and throw rubber rings at it.

'One euro for three throws,' I said. 'If you get a ring around a hook you get a special prize.'

'Which is what?'

'Something from the gadget box.'

The gadget box was full of old pencil toppers, erasers, keyrings and other junk. Another brilliant idea of mine.

'Okay,' said Nicholas, 'but where does the board go?'

'What do you mean?'

'Where are you going to hang the board?'

Ah. I hadn't thought of that. In the driveway there was no wall to hang anything on.

Nicholas was giving me an 'oh dear, you messed up' look, so I picked up the board and walked slowly around the table, acting like it was obvious where it should go. I could lean it against something in front of the table, but that would be too low. I could try and balance it on top of the pillar, but it was bound to fall over. In the end I walked a full circle around the table, then stood behind it, smiling.

'Well?' said Nicholas. 'Where does the board go?'

'Right here,' I said.

'Where?'

'Here.' I held the board in front of me. 'Have a go.'

'You're just going to stand there holding it? For the whole Jumble Sale?'

'Well ... yes, obviously. You guys do the selling and I'll run the hoop game. Simple.'

Nicholas threw one of the rubber rings and it hit me in the face.

'Are you totally, absolutely sure you want to hold it?' he said.

'Yes,' I said, smiling while I ground my teeth, 'I'm sure.'

'Okay then.'

It was ten past two, we'd had no customers yet and my arms were aching.

'What's taking so long?' said Lex.

'Dunno,' I said, 'but I'm sure– ... Lex! Have you been at the jellies again?'

Pause.

'No.'

'For goodness sake!'

I put down the hoop board, grabbed the jelly jar, tipped the sweets into the biscuit tin, counted them and put them back. It took *ages*. And Lex had definitely been at them. There were four fewer than before.

'Is this it?'

While I'd been busy counting sweets, a customer had finally shown up. Unfortunately it was Sasha Noonan – evil snob extraordinaire – and she was squishing up her face like our Jumble Sale was something smelly.

'It's just a load of junk,' she said. 'Why

would anyone buy this stuff when they can go the toy shop in town and get something *new*.'

'Because some people,' I said, 'prefer to buy toys that have a history, toys with *character*.'

'What does that even mean?'

I wasn't sure, but I tried to look at Sasha the way the woman running the antique shop had looked at me. I stood up really tall, half-closed my eyes and said in a really posh voice, 'I could explain it but I really don't think you'd understand.'

Sasha snorted. 'Whatever. Losers.'

She walked off and we didn't have to wait long for our next customer. It was one of the small kids from our street – Jennifer Mullally – and her mum.

'Hi, Mrs Mullally,' I said, grabbing up the hoop board. 'Hi, Jennifer. Would you like to have a go at the hoop game? Only one euro for three throws.'

Jennifer went all shy and held on to her mum's jeans.

'No thanks, Cass,' said Mrs Mullally.

'No problem,' Nicholas said, smiling. 'How about a toy instead? Feel free to browse.'

'Oh,' Mrs Mullally said, glancing over the table. 'It's, em ... lovely.'

'I want that, Mammy.'

Jennifer was pointing to a doll that was just a head and shoulders; it was one of those ones you can practise makeup and hairstyles on.

'But, sweetie,' Mrs Mullally said, 'all the hair's been cut off.'

'But I like it.'

'And someone's drawn all over the face with markers.'

'But I like it.'

'I don't think so, sweetheart.'

'But I *like* it.'

'How about this one, Jennifer?' Nicholas said, holding up another doll.

'It's got no eyes,' Mrs Mullally said, 'and it looks very worn.'

'It is very old. In fact, it's vintage. You can't get dolls like these anymore.'

Vintage. Nicholas was a genius. But genius or not, Mrs Mullally wasn't having any of it.

In the end, she let Jennifer have a couple of guesses at how many sweets were in the jar (Jennifer can't count yet, so she guessed five and a hundred), and bought her a troll pencil topper from the gadget box. It wasn't much money for us.

'One euro and thirty cents?' said Nicholas. 'That doesn't even cover the cost of the jellies.'

'Relax,' I said, 'the day's not over yet.'

But Jennifer turned out to be our last customer. By the time we gave up I'd been holding the hoop board for so long I couldn't feel my arms anymore.

Chapter Five

I was very down in the dumps. Our Jumble Sale had been a disaster, we still had no money to pay for Nicholas's masterclass and, to top it all off, I was still being outsmarted by the invisible boy.

I hadn't forgotten about my solo mission to reveal the boy in our class that none of us could see. At lunchtime, after we'd all finished our sandwiches, everybody filed out to the yard to play. Mr Freebs was on yard duty so he left as well. I stayed in my seat, staring at the empty chair on the very left of the front row. Invisible Boy hadn't gone out with the others – I could sense that he was there

– so I decided now was time for a little chat, when there was no one in the classroom but me and him.

'I know you're there,' I said.

Nothing.

'And you're probably not going to talk to me because you're really sneaky, and I think you like people thinking that that's just an empty chair you're sitting in.'

Still nothing. I sighed.

'Fine. You may not want to talk to me, but I'm going to talk to you. Because I'm having a terrible week. And I can't really talk to my friends because if I do they'll know that Operation Start a Company has failed.' I narrowed my eyes at Invisible Boy. 'That's a secret mission name. Don't go telling anyone else that.' Invisible Boy didn't respond and I was starting to think we had an understanding. 'I'm the CEO of the company, see? It's my job to make sure it's a success. But I think I'm letting Lex and Nicholas down because I haven't got any more good ideas. I don't think we're going to be millionaires after all.'

Invisible Boy didn't say anything. He just stared at me like I was being ridiculous (at least, I think he did).

'It's not easy, you know,' I snapped. 'I mean, I've got a brilliant brain and I'm deadly at solving puzzles and working things out, but this is just too hard.'

He still didn't say anything. He's so *annoying*.

'Fine then,' I said, losing my temper. 'I *will* have another great idea, and I *will* make sure Nicholas goes to his masterclass, and the

Bubble Street Gang company *will* be a success. I'll show you.'

I stood up and marched to the door. Before leaving, I turned around.

'You know, you're not so bad, Invisible Boy. I kind of feel bad that I'm going to expose you and your supernatural power to the whole world. Oh, well.' I walked out, but popped my head back around the door jamb. 'And don't you dare tell *anyone* the name of our secret club. It's a secret.'

I went out into the yard feeling much better. The sun was shining and my brain was turning like a great big machine. I was going to have another brilliant idea. I could feel it.

'Who were you talking to?'

Nathan Wall, with his terrible greasy hair,

stood in front of me and blocked out the sunshine.

'What?' I said. 'What are you talking about?'

'Sasha was passing the classroom and she heard you talking. But there was no one else in there. So who were you talking to?'

Sasha Noonan and Jim Brick stood behind Nathan and giggled. The three of them make up the Na-Sa-Ji Club (that's the first two letters of each of their names – *terrible* name for a club). It's supposed to be a secret club, like the Bubble Street Gang, except that me and Lex and Nicholas found out about it during our last adventure. We didn't tell them we found out about it though. We let them have their secret. Sometimes I wish we hadn't.

'You were talking to yourself, weren't you?'

Nathan said with a big grin. 'Cass Okara's so weird – she talks to *herself!*'

He said the last bit really loudly, so the whole yard would hear, and Sasha and Jim laughed harder. It made me angry, but I should have just felt sorry for them. The Na-Sa-Ji Club have tiny, tiny minds. There's a girl talking to an empty room, and they immediately assume she's talking to herself? I would never assume that.

Definition of assume: to decide something about something before you've got all the information. Like a snobby member of the snobby Na-Sa-Ji Club would do.

A genius detective must never assume anything – they must have big, open minds so they can let in all the information; soak up all the facts, like a sponge.

Someone talking to an empty room might be talking to themselves. Or they might be talking to an invisible person (like I was); they could be talking to someone hiding in the cupboard; they could be talking to a talking bird outside the window; they could be speaking to a creature in another dimension through a portal in the ceiling; they could be talking to a recording device hidden in the desk, or a microphone in the wall ...

There are *so many* possibilities. But Nathan and his snobby friends could only think of one. They really have such tiny, tiny minds.

I pushed past them into the yard, smiling

to myself. I wouldn't let them get me down, because I'd just come up with another brilliant idea.

Chapter Six

BUBBLE TOURS

Discover fascinating facts about your

local area

Take a virtual holiday in a far off land

Also, there's a Ghost Tour

For more information contact

Cass Okara, 25 Berbel Street.

Please note, Bubble Tours takes no responsibility for

lost bags, sunglasses or people.

'Bubble Tours?' Nicholas said.

He held up the poster I'd made and read it aloud.

'This,' I said, 'is what's gonna get you into your masterclass. It's genius.'

It was genius. I don't know why I hadn't thought of it before.

Do you know all about the place where you live? I bet you think you do, but I bet you really don't. I know way more than normal people about the place I live, because I'm a detective. I have a detective's mind, so I don't just wander around thinking, *Hmm, that's a nice garden* or *Look, a new sweet shop*. I go much deeper. I investigate. I can't help it, it's my curious mind.

For example, Mr Dixon's back garden is a nice garden, but did you know that he copied Mrs Leadbetter's front garden? Well, he did. One row of yellow daffodils, one row of purple flowers (don't know what they're called), one row of white ones and, behind them all, a water feature that looks like a pile of pebbles, *exactly* the same pile of pebbles. Check them out if you don't believe me. No one has noticed because nobody's allowed into Mr Dixon's back garden. I was in there once because ... well, it was this whole thing to do with his cat, but I won't go into that right now. So, where a normal person might walk past Mrs Leadbetter's house thinking, *Hmm, that's a nice garden*, I'm thinking, *Hmm, Mr Dixon's a copycat.*

That's where I got the idea for Bubble Tours. We have a number of tours available, but the main event is the Berbel Street Tour. It's the best one. It's where I show you all the hidden mysteries and fascinating secrets of what looks like an ordinary, sleepy street.

After finishing our first ever Berbel Street Tour, I decided that it was no longer our main event. Mr Manning had been our first customer. We asked him first because he's the nicest man alive and never says 'no' to anything. At one point during the tour, though, he came as close to saying 'no' as I'd ever heard him.

'Will we move on to the next stop on the tour?' I said.

'Oh, well … em … I don't know. Do *you* want to keep going with the tour?'

I showed him the dent in the tarmac that my head had made when I fell off my bike for the first time. I told him that Mrs McCourt and Ms Lee had a fenderbender (that means they crashed cars, but only a little bit) nearly a year ago and became mortal enemies. I told him about the Smyths' dog sneaking into the Noonans' house and stealing an entire cooked chicken off the kitchen table and Mr Noonan threatening to sue. I even got desperate and told him about the invisible boy in my class, and nothing! Not so much as a raised eyebrow from Mr Manning.

I gave up. I decided the Berbel Street Tour wasn't the right one for him. He needed a break from the street; an exotic holiday on a white sandy beach, with the sun beating down and the gentle sound of ocean waves in the background. He needed the Bubble Tours *Virtual Holiday*.

Imagine this: You're lying on a beach on a desert island in the middle of the Pacific Ocean. The bright yellow sun is shining down on you, but there's also a cool breeze. You can hear the *shush-shush* of the waves on the sand and the caw-caw of the birds in the sky. Nice, isn't it?

That's what it's like when you're on a Bubble Tours virtual holiday. You are totally, totally relaxed.

Mr Manning was not totally, totally relaxed. I don't know why. We were simulating the desert island experience perfectly.

He sat in his front garden in a reclining patio chair that we had dragged all the way from Nicholas's house. With the clever use of extension cords, I was holding a blow heater over his face to simulate the heat of the sun and Lex was holding a fan near the back of his head to simulate a cool breeze. Next to me, Nicholas stood holding up a gigantic poster of a white beach with palm trees and blue water splashing onto the sand. There was even a little row boat on one side that made it look really real.

Nicholas was making the sound of the waves by going, '*Whoosh*-sh-sh-sh-sh, *whoosh*-sh-sh-sh-sh' over and over again, and I was doing a deadly impression of bird calls by going, 'caw-caw-caw'. I was really good at it too. I did quiet ones, <small>'caw-caw-caw'</small> to sound like birds that were far away, and I did loud ones, **'CAW-CAW-CAW'** to sound like birds that were really close. Sometimes Mr Manning jumped at the loud ones.

No matter how brilliant our desert island

experience was, Mr Manning wouldn't sit still and relax. He jumped and fidgeted and kept brushing back his hair when Lex's fan blew it forward and into his eyes.

'Mr Manning,' I said finally, 'you're on holiday. You're supposed to relax and enjoy the sunshine.'

'That heater's very close,' he said, wiping sweat from his forehead, 'I think it's burning me.'

'Of course!' I said. 'I forgot the sunscreen. Hang on 'til I go get some. My mum's got a coconut one that smells like summer.'

'No, no, no,' Mr Manning said, brushing back his hair again. 'I think I ... eh ... I think I should get back inside. I meant to water the house plants today, so I must get on with that. Thanks very much for the– Ow!'

He had leaned back too far while trying to get off the reclining patio chair and his hair got caught in the fan.

'Ow, ow, ow, ow!'

'Oh, sorry!' Lex cried.

She tried to untangle his hair with one hand, but the fan was still going.

'Turn it off, Lex!' I said.

'I'm trying!'

The off-switch was on the side of the fan and Lex couldn't reach it. She was holding the base of the fan with one hand, and a whole lot of Mr Manning's hair with the other (trying to stop it getting more and more twisted in the blades that were spinning around so fast).

'Ow, ow, ow, ow, ow!' Mr Manning cried.

'Don't worry,' I said, 'I'm on it!'

I sprang into action by dropping the heater (which landed on Mr Manning's foot), grabbing hold of the fan (accidentally pressing the *Turbo* button, which made the blades spin even faster) and, when Mr Manning shrieked in pain and rolled off the side of the chair pulling the fan with him by his hair, I dropped the fan too (which landed on his head).

Poor Mr Manning. He was bruised all over. And when we finally untangled him from the fan there was a clump of silky white hair left wrapped around the blades.

'I'm so sorry, Mr Manning,' I said as we helped him to his front door. 'Please let us make it up to you. How about a nice, relaxing cruise around the Arctic Circle? My auntie's got one of those big freezers–'

'*NO!*' He held out his hands for a second, then gave me a smile that looked forced. 'No, no, no, that's all right, kids. You've been very good, but I'd ... I'd like to go inside and sit down for a while. I don't think virtual holidaying is for me. Best of luck with it all.'

'Wow,' Lex said as we collected up our gear and walked down the driveway. 'Mr Manning never says no.'

'I guess he really didn't like our virtual holiday experience,' said Nicholas.

'Yeah,' I said, 'some people just don't know how to relax.'

Don't think for a second that I was giving up on Bubble Tours so easily. So the Berbel Street Tour was not a complete success; so the Virtual Holiday ended with a broken heater and some loss of hair. Mistakes are how you learn. And so far the Bubble Street Gang had learned *loads*.

The Ghost Tour was going to be the money-maker, and not only that, it was going to be so much *fun* making up ghost stories and planning scary things to jump out at people.

Yes, you read that right, we were planning to *make up* ghost stories. You see, the thing is, there aren't really any ghost stories in Berbel Street or any haunted places around where we live (except for the empty house opposite Nicholas's house. That's actually haunted. But not in a fun way, more in a scary don't-go-in-there-or-a-ghost-will-eat-you kind of way. We do NOT go near the empty house). We all asked our parents if they knew about any ghosts in Berbel Street, but they were no help at all – they didn't even know the empty house was haunted. We checked online at school (Mr Freebs helped us search), but there were no results for 'Berbel Street + ghost story'. We even went to the library and took out a bunch of books on the town and local area, but we couldn't find one single story about a real-life ghost. There were no ghosts in Berbel Street. The Ghost Tour was going to be a bust.

Then it hit me; how did we know for sure there were no ghosts in Berbel Street? After all, ghosts are invisible (like the boy in my class) and they're quiet (when they want to be). In all the books I've ever read about ghosts, they're usually being loud and jumping out because they're mad at somebody, or because they're trying to keep people away from their treasure. There could be a whole load of ghosts out there that aren't angry and don't have any treasure; quiet ghosts who just go for walks and ignore people all day. Berbel Street could be jammers with ghosts. We had no way of knowing. So couldn't we imagine what those ghosts might be like and then tell stories about them?

It turns out, yes we can. I asked my dad about making up fun stories about things that might be true, and he said something about 'artistic license'. He went on for ages about it and used some really big words, but I've made his explanation much simpler here:

Definition of artistic license: an artist (that's anybody who does arty things like writing or drawing or making up stories) is allowed to make up or change things in order to make them better (or more entertaining).

Apparently lots of famous artists do it so it's totally okay.

'We're going to make up fake ghosts?' Nicholas said as we munched on cookies in the clubhouse.

'Not *fake* ghosts,' I said. 'For all we know these ghosts really exist. They're just really ... quiet, and we don't know what they're like. So we're going to *imagine* what they're like.'

Lex was taking the minutes of the company meeting on her mini laptop again. She shivered.

'I don't like ghosts.'

'Well don't worry,' I said, 'we'll be the ones doing all the scaring.'

'What do you mean?'

'There'll be ghost stories on the Ghost Tour and, every now and then, a ghost is going to pop out and go, *RAARRRR!*'

I made an angry ghost face and Lex nearly fell off her chair.

'Don't do that!'

'Sorry. But the people on the tour are going to love it.'

'Wait,' said Nicholas, 'you mean we'll have to dress up?'

'Of course.'

If a human face could actually light up like a light bulb, that's exactly what Nicholas's face would have done.

Chapter Seven

Operation Invisible Boy: Update

Saw Star Wars comic on Invisible Boy's desk. Deduced (that means worked out) that Invisible Boy likes Star Wars. Decided to force Invisible Boy to speak by pretending to know nothing about Star Wars (really, really loudly) at lunchtime.

Me: 'Nicholas, I love the way Han Solo in Star Wars is really good at fighting with a lightsaber.'

Nicholas: 'Huh?'

Me: 'And did you know that Chewbacca is actually Bigfoot, and that all the Ewoks are his babies?'

Nicholas: 'Cass, are you all right?'

Could almost feel Invisible Boy's head about to explode. Kept going.

Me: 'And I love the way Princess Leia wore actual Danish pastries in her hair because they're the official breakfast of Alderaan.'

Annoying voice from back of the room: 'What?! What are you talking about? You know nothing about Star Wars. Han Solo used a blaster, not a lightsaber – he wasn't a Jedi – and Chewbacca's not related to the Ewoks, he's a Wookiee. And Princess Leia didn't have Danish pastries on her head! You're so stupid, Cass.'

I HATE YOU, NATHAN WALL!!

Plan foiled by evil, snobby class-mate. Invisible Boy escapes me once again. Sad face.

'Papa's got a head like a ping pong ball, Papa's got a head like a ping pong ball, Papa's got a head like a ping pong ball, juuuust like a ping pong ball.'

Nicholas was warming up for the big Ghost Tour performance. His mouth was opening and closing so fast he looked like a hyper goldfish that had eaten too much sugar.

'Plapa's like a head with a ping pang ba– ... no, Parpa's in a place with the ping pong wall ... wait ...'

Lex couldn't keep up. She kept tripping over her words. I don't think she likes tongue twisters anyway, but even if she did she was so nervous it wouldn't have made any difference. Nicholas had been really patient at first – going over all the rhymes with her really slowly – and he'd picked the Papa one because there's a tune to it so it's like a little song. He thought it would help. It did not help.

'Pingy's in the pop with the head-thing on ... no, no, wait ...'

'Lex,' Nicholas cried, 'that's not even close.'

'I'm trying!

'Well, you'll have to try harder. You can't perform in front of all those people without properly warming up.'

Lex went green. At least I think she did, it was hard to tell under all that white makeup.

'I think I'm gonna be ...'

She ran out of Nicholas's room and we heard the bathroom door slam shut.

It's weird. I've seen Lex climb trees so high they would make monkeys weak at the knees. I've seen her dangle from the rafters in the school hall without so much as blinking. I've watched her crawl out her bedroom window, shimmy down the drainpipe and leap onto the roof of the garden shed. None of that stuff bothers her at all. She's like a girl without fear.

But ask her to say two words in front of people she doesn't know and her legs turn to jelly.

'Cass,' Nicholas turned to me, 'you're up.'

'Why do I have to do tongue twisters? I'm not performing, I'm the tour guide.'

'The tour guide is a performer. From the

moment you open your mouth the audience should feel like they're at a show. You've got to hold their attention.'

I don't usually have any trouble getting people's attention, but I sighed and said,

'Fine.'

'Good. Now repeat after me. Red lorry, yellow lorry, red lorry, yellow lorry ...'

'Red lorry, yellow lolly, red lully, lellow lully–'

'No, no, no, no! Listen to yourself as you say it. It's red ... lorry ... yellow ... lorry ...'

He was speaking really, really slowly and looking at me like I was a dim-witted puppy.

'I know what the words are, Nicholas.'

'Then say them.'

I huffed out a breath and tried again.

'Red lorry, yellow lorry, red lorry, yellow

lorry,' it was going very well so Nicholas turned his hand in the air to signal me to speed up, 'red lorry, yellow lorry, red-lorry-yellow-lorry-red-lolly-yellow-lolly-red-lully-rellow-rolley-red-rurry-rellow-lully–'

'No, no, no, no!'

'Oh forget it, I'll be grand without it.'

'You have to warm up so you can talk properly during the tour.'

'I know how to *talk*, Nicholas.'

He shook his head at me and I knew he was thinking that I was such an amateur. That's because Nicholas takes acting *way* too seriously. Sometimes it's fun, like when we're playing games and he has to act like there is a monster invading the town and it's really convincing. But other times, like this time, it's just really, really annoying.

I couldn't stay mad at him for long though, because Lex came out of the bathroom and her makeup still looked awesome. So did Nicholas's. He really is very good at costumes and makeup.

Lex was what he called a 'mournful ghost.' Her hair was tied back really tight (which already looked weird because Lex never ties her hair back) and her face was really white and pasty, with shadows around her eyes and in her cheeks so she looked gaunt and like a skeleton. Nicholas had

taken an old shirt and trousers, and ripped and muddied them so it looked like Lex had been buried for years. It looked like she'd crawled right out of a grave – it was *awesome*.

Nicholas was what he called a 'malevolent ghost'. He must have looked up that word, because I had to ask my mum what it meant.

Definition of malevolent:
really, really bold.

He'd used this hairspray stuff that made his hair black, then he'd drawn a big toothy grin from one side of his face to the other, so it looked like his mouth was gigantic. He'd wanted to wear red contacts too, to make his eyes look red, but his mum said he was too young. He'll be allowed use them when he's fifteen. *Ages* away.

The 'malevolent ghost' didn't look like he'd been buried at all. He was in a really smart suit with a tie and everything, and a long black cloak like a vampire would wear. I argued that he should have been in rags too, but after I saw the whole costume with the face paint I had to admit it worked really well.

It worked so well that looking at Nicholas was kind of freaking me out.

'Don't stare,' I said. 'It makes your face look even weirder.'

'You mean scarier?' he said, wriggling his fingers at me.

'It's not me you're supposed to be scaring. Save it for the tour.'

I wouldn't let on, but he really was scaring me a little bit.

We'd told everybody that the Ghost Tour started at twilight (cos it sounded very cool and mysterious), but that meant loads of kids kept calling to our houses asking when twilight was.

'Sunset,' I said to another kid at Nicholas's door, 'about half six.'

'*About* half six, or half six?' the boy said. 'I'm not standing in the road waiting for ages.'

'Half six then,' I snapped. 'Tell the others.'

It was half five already and Nicholas's dad was making us something to eat in the kitchen.

'Wow!' he said, when Nicholas and Lex walked in. 'Those are a couple of seriously brilliant costumes, you guys.'

'Thanks, Dad,' said Nicholas, sitting down at the table.

It was freaky hearing nice, polite words coming out of Nicholas's big, nasty grin.

'So,' his dad said, putting bowls of tomato soup on the table, 'a ghost tour, eh? Brilliant idea.'

'My idea,' I said. 'But I knew Nicholas could do some deadly costumes for it.'

'And he certainly did. You kids are gonna knock 'em dead. Ha! Knock 'em dead. That's funny.'

Nicholas's dad chuckled to himself as we all grabbed toasted cheese sandwiches from a plate in the middle of the table. While we were eating, I couldn't help thinking of Invisible Boy. What an awesome addition to the Ghost Tour he would have made! He could have run around the tour group, pinching people's arms and pulling at their

hair, and they would have freaked out –
'Who's doing that? What is that? All I can
see is empty air. Aaaaaah!'

I sighed. It was a shame I hadn't managed
to reveal him yet. I made a mental note to
get back to my solo investigation as soon as
the Ghost Tour was over.

When we'd finished eating we had a hard
time convincing Nicholas's dad that he
couldn't come and watch us perform.

'But can't I go on the tour as well?' he
asked. 'I'll buy a ticket.'

'All booked up,' I said.

'Anyway,' said Nicholas, 'there's only kids
on this tour. It'd ruin it for them if an adult
came along. Maybe next time, Dad.'

His dad looked so disappointed.

'Oh, okay then. Well, break a leg, you lot.'

With Nicholas and Lex holding coats over their heads to hide their makeup, we headed out into the street. It was only a quarter past six, but the other two had to get out early to get to their hiding places. Our tour guests had no idea what was in store for them!

Chapter Eight

To say that the Ghost Tour went perfectly would not quite be true. To say it went badly would not be true either. To say that it went really, really well *and* really, really badly would be just about right.

'This is all your fault,' Nicholas whispered to me as we sat in the sitting room in my house, waiting for our parents.

His makeup was all messy. He'd tried to wipe off most of the big grin before we sat down.

Lex was sitting on the other side of him. Her eyes were all red, but not from the makeup. From the crying. And the crying was not because we were in trouble, but because she'd scared *herself* so badly. Sound weird? It was a bit. Let me sum it all up for you.

The tour began on the street outside my house. I was there before any of the tour guests arrived, standing on the path looking all serious and mysterious. It was twilight (that time of day when the sun is setting and the light gets all eerie) and it was perfect.

'Before we begin,' I said to the kids standing around me (there were about twelve of them, all different ages), 'I must warn you that this tour will scare the daylights out of you. It may even scare the *life* out of you. But Bubble Tours cannot be held responsible. You're taking this tour at your own risk.'

'Ooh,' Bianca said, waving her hands,

'we're so scared.'

Why was Bianca there at all? There was no one else on the tour her age; no one else who was already in big school. Talking in front of a thirteen-year-old made me feel silly and childish. But I wouldn't be put off. I was going to make her jump if it was the last thing I did.

I smiled a wicked smile and gestured for everyone to follow me.

'The first stop on our tour,' I said, 'is the house of Mr Dixon. Not many people know this but there is something terrifying trapped in the ...'

I was supposed to say 'attic' – it was a ghost story I'd made up earlier – but Bianca was doing lots of smirking and fake yawning, so I came up with something better. In the driveway of the house sat Mr Dixon's cat, Bless. I usually do not like Mr Dixon's cat – he's a huge ball of white and orange fur that stands in your way and glares at you like you're an idiot. But, for once, I was happy to see him.

'... There is something terrifying trapped in the body of *Mr Dixon's cat*,' I said.

There were gasps and moans, and somebody's little brother grabbed on to his big sister's arm.

'That's right, people. Mr Dixon's cat is actually a *werewolf*. And during every full moon he grows into a snarling beast that prowls the streets looking for someone to eat.' I clawed my hands and growled.

'Wolves are like dogs,' Bianca sneered. 'Why would a cat be a werewolf?'

'I meant were-*cat*,' I said. 'He's a werecat,

all right? So beware, everybody, when that cat stands in the middle of the path and stares you down, it might just be picking you out as its next midnight meal.'

Mr Dixon's cat was very obliging and continued to sit and stare at everybody with sleepy, sneaky eyes. All the kids (except for pain-in-my-bum Bianca) looked really scared. Brilliant.

The next stop on the tour was where things got a bit wobbly. Lex was hiding in a tree outside Mrs McCourt's house. She was to be the mournful ghost of Mrs McCourt's car, still upset about the little car crash with Ms Lee. When I said the magic word – fender-bender – Lex was to drop into view, swinging upside down from a branch by her knees and howling like a banshee. And she did just

that. And it was wonderful. For about half a second.

Lex has never fallen off anything in her life. She's climbed trees and walls and lampposts and drainpipes, and she never falls. But this time she did.

I think it was a mixture of things; she was really nervous, which made her legs a bit shaky; she was wearing a pair of torn, baggy trousers that really didn't fit her; and, most of all, when she dropped into view she caught sight of her own reflection in the window of Mrs McCourt's car, which was parked next to the tree. For a moment, she thought she was looking at the *real* mournful ghost of Mrs McCourt's car, and it scared her so much she fell right out of the tree. Onto this one kid, Barry.

Some other kids thought the ghost was attacking him and trying to eat him and they ran away screaming. Barry himself wasn't badly hurt, but he was crying, so his sister took him home. Lex had a graze on her forehead and was still shaky after scaring herself, so she went home too.

The tour went on, but it had gotten much, much smaller.

For the final stop on the tour I took the group to the laneway that runs alongside Mr McCall's field. Nicholas was hiding behind the fence on the other side. The plan was that, while I told a brilliant story about the 'Phantom in the Field', he would creep slowly across the grass, keeping his face covered with the cloak. People would notice and start pointing him out and I'd pretend like

I couldn't see him and then, when he was close enough, he'd throw off his cloak and roar with his big painted grin.

That's not quite what happened.

It was starting to get dark, so the scene was perfect. I could just about see Nicholas crouched down in the corner at the other side of the field. We were all set.

I started telling the story of the 'Phantom in the Field', adding in lots of gruesome details and scary bits. Everybody was hanging on my every word. Out of the corner of my eye I saw something black start moving towards us.

Brilliant, I thought. *This is going perfectly.*

But then, out of the other corner of my eye, I saw something brown start moving towards us.

'What's that?' someone said, pointing to the black thing.

'What's that?' someone else said, pointing to the brown thing.

The brown thing was moving quicker now, and it was on a collision course with Nicholas. Suddenly, I realised what it was.

'Nicholas!' I yelled. 'There's a bull in the field!'

This was not the first time there'd been a bull in Mr McCall's field. There was one there when we were building our clubhouse. That bull had seemed quite calm and quiet. This new bull did not seem calm and quiet. It huffed and puffed smoky air from its nose as it ran.

'Run, Nicholas, ruuuun!' I screamed.

Nicholas was running properly now, his

cloak thrown back over his shoulder. The kids on the tour kept pointing and yelling and looking to me – I think they thought it was part of the show – and it wasn't until Nicholas launched himself over the fence, with his cloak billowing out behind him like bat wings, and his huge painted grin horrible in the darkness, that they all screamed and screamed and screamed and started running.

Nicholas landed in a heap at my feet and, without a word, I grabbed him and started running too. I didn't think a bull could jump over a fence, but I wasn't taking any chances.

So the tour was terrifying for everybody (the Bubble Street Gang included); so terrifying that lots of parents rang up our parents to give out. And that's how me and Lex and Nicholas ended up in my sitting room, kind of in trouble.

Our parents said that the Ghost Tour was very 'creative' and 'innovative' and 'interesting', but that we were never, ever, *ever*, to do it again.

'At least we gave Bianca a good scare,' I whispered to Nicholas.

'Yeah,' he whispered back, smiling, 'I think she screamed even louder than you did.'

Chapter Nine

Operation Invisible Boy: Update

New plan: pretend to trip and fall
next to Invisible Boy's desk. Pretend
to cry as well so he'll feel bad and
help me up.

Tried to pretend to trip and fall
near Invisible Boy's desk. Actually
tripped and fell instead. Actually
cried a bit too. Knee very hurt.
Invisible Boy did not help me up or
say anything or do anything
nice at all.

Getting seriously sick and tired of
Invisible Boy.

It was really quiet in the clubhouse. Me and Lex sat at the table and didn't talk. We were feeling pretty low. We didn't even have any cookies to munch on and make us feel better. Distracted by all the company stuff, we'd been neglecting the clubhouse. Rule No. 6 of the clubhouse:

6. Members will take turns to refill the snack jars.

It was my turn and I'd totally forgotten about it. Now we had nothing to eat. According to the clubhouse rules (which I wrote) I was supposed to be punished. That meant sitting in the naughty corner wearing a jester's hat. But, between the tour failure and my solo investigation getting nowhere, I was too sad to sit in the naughty corner, and Lex was too sad to make me.

The door opened and Nicholas came in.

'You're late for the club meeting,' I said, though I didn't really care.

'I had to take the long way,' he replied. 'I think that bull remembers me from the Ghost Tour. He keeps staring at me and snorting.'

'Well, you're here now so I guess we should start the meeting.'

I noticed Lex didn't bother to open her laptop.

'Can I grab a cookie first?' said Nicholas.

'There aren't any,' I said.

After a minute Nicholas sat down and we all stared at the table and said nothing. Finally, I sighed.

'I'm sorry, Nicholas. We're not going to make enough money to send you to the costume masterclass.'

'What about the money from the Ghost Tour?'

'There wasn't enough. Besides, mum made me give it all back to the kids on the street, as a sorry for scaring the life out of them.'

'Oh.'

I could tell he was trying not to look too disappointed, but he wasn't that good an actor.

'I'm really sorry, Nicholas.'

'That's okay. Thanks for trying. It was really nice of you both.'

'The Bubble Street Gang sticks together, huh?'

'Yeah,' he said.

'Yeah,' said Lex.

We meant it, but we were too sad to cheer. I leaned over and picked up Lex's laptop. I opened the minutes document and read it. The start looked like this:

OPERATION START A COMPANY AND MAKE LOADS OF MONEY FOR NICHOLAS'S MASTERCLASS AND PROBABLY ALSO BECOME MILLIONAIRES

FIRST COMPANY MEETING

- Need to come up with plan for making loads of money.
- Did not come up with plan for making loads of money.

Most of the updates underneath were just as bad.

- Jennifer Mullally's older sister, Aisling, complained that jar of sweets from Jumble Sale was short 46 jellies (Jennifer was only player, so she won. Cass had written '132 jellies' on inside of lid when they were first counted. Aisling too clever and found it). Lex to buy replacement jellies with next week's pocket money. And probably the week after's as well.

• Blow heater that we used for Mr Manning's Virtual Tour is definitely broken. Nicholas wants it on the record that he is not happy. His room is really cold.

• For any future Ghost Tours, make sure to check beforehand for any dangerous wildlife in fields etc. Also, there will be no future Ghost Tours because they are banned.

• Current balance: €0.00 (minus the money we spent, which was a lot)

I took a deep breath and sighed loudly. Then underneath it all, in giant letters, I typed,

OPERATION STATUS:
FAILED

We were all hungry and bored so we left

the clubhouse and crossed the plank bridge over the stream to walk the long way home.

'Ah, look who it is!'

Lex's granny sat on a fold-out chair in front of the granny clubhouse, with a cup of tea in one hand and one of her thriller novels in the other. She grinned at us like a fiendish owl in her over-sized sunglasses.

Me and Lex and Nicholas built the granny clubhouse in the hedge, a few trees down from our own place, after we discovered Mrs Brooks and her friends had been invading *our* clubhouse. You might think it's terrible having a bunch of elderly adults nearby, but actually it's all right. They never bother us unless they've got a scavenger hunt or a riddle for us to solve, which is good practice for our investigating skills. Also, Lex's granny is the coolest adult I know. Actually, she's diabolical; very wicked and very clever, and kind of my role model.

'Quitting the clubhouse a little early today, aren't you, Bubble Street Gang?' she said.

'We're too hungry, Gran,' Lex said, 'there's no food left.'

'And we don't deserve the clubhouse today,' I said, 'because we're great big failures.'

'My, my,' Lex's granny said, sitting up and whipping off her sunglasses, 'that doesn't sound like the feisty gang I know and love. Come in, have a cup of tea, and tell me all about it.'

She vanished into the granny clubhouse but we didn't follow. We hadn't been inside since we built the place; it felt like we would be invading. Lex's granny popped her head out the door.

'I've got those mini muffins with the vanilla cream in the middle. Want some? Speak now or forever hold your peace.'

'We want some!' Lex yelled, and we all trooped over the granny-plank-bridge and inside.

There's something slightly eerie about the granny clubhouse. I mean, it's newer than our clubhouse, but it smells musty and old. And there are loads of ornaments and porcelain angels piled on shelves. How did they make it feel so old so quickly?

Lex's granny boiled the kettle on the camp stove, and laid out some mini muffins on a doily in the middle of the table. We gobbled them down before the tea was even ready.

'Which means,' I said through a mouthful

of muffin, after we'd told her the whole story, 'that our very first company was a complete and total disaster.'

'Yes, yes,' said Lex's granny, sipping her tea, 'I see what you mean.'

'What do you mean, you see what we mean?' asked Nicholas.

She shrugged. 'Your company is a total disaster. You've failed miserably. Come to think of it, I don't think you deserved those mini muffins.'

We sat there and stared in shock. That was way harsh!

'Hang on a minute,' I said. 'I know what you're doing. You're trying to make us angry so we'll tell you that we're *not* failures and that we're going to go out and make this company a success, no matter what you say.'

Lex's granny narrowed her eyes. 'You're always a quick one, Cass.'

'So we do deserve the mini muffins?' Lex said, with the last bite of the last muffin hovering by her mouth.

Her granny sat up and put her cup on the table.

'Do you know my friend Mabel is awful at poker? Really, she's terrible. She loses every game. She can't bluff for toffee and I can read her like a book.'

'So?' said Nicholas.

'So, do you think Mabel quits playing poker?'

'Yes.'

'No!'

'Well, she should.'

'Why?' Lex's granny said. 'Because she's

not good at it? So what? She likes to play. Sure, she gets frustrated and annoyed and she accuses me of cheating – which I never would, by the way. I don't have to with Mabel – but she keeps on playing–'

'Because she has a good time,' said Lex.

'Yes, because she has a good time. Sure, it'd be nice to win a pot of money at the end, but it's the game that matters – the *journey*. That's the best part.' Lex's granny picked up her tea again and sat back. 'Besides, she's determined to beat me one of these days, and you know what? She tries so hard I think she just might. One of these days.'

'So you think we should keep on trying,' I said. 'You think we should try something else to make the money for Nicholas's masterclass.'

'I think you kids are capable of *anything* if you put your minds to it,' Lex's granny said. 'But even if you don't make enough money for the masterclass, do you really want to miss out on the adventure you might have in trying? Is winning the game really the only thing that matters?'

I smiled. 'Maybe we'll have one more go.'

'Yeah,' said Lex, grinning.

'I'm in!' said Nicholas.

Lex's granny winked. 'That's the Bubble Street Gang I know and love.'

Chapter Ten

It was horrible. My bedroom – a brilliant place full of movie posters and books and detective equipment – totally destroyed.

'*Muuuum!*'

The annoying baby twins had got in. Pippi and Ade, the mini-monsters I am forced to share the house with, got into my room and wrecked it.

'*Muuuum!*' I yelled, while Lex and Nicholas picked their way through the wreckage.

'What is it, Cass?' came my mum's voice from downstairs.

'The twins wrecked my room.'

'Did you leave the door open?'

'No, I did not!'

When there's a girl in the house who'll chew the legs off a table, and a boy who'll sneeze a gallon of snot over everything you own, you learn to keep your bedroom door shut.

'I'll help you clean up later,' my mum called.

'But we need the room *now*.'

'That's enough shouting, Cass. Come downstairs and talk like a normal person.'

I stomped downstairs, huffing and snarling and complaining, and after my mum had given me the usual lecture – 'They're only two years old, Cass, they didn't mean any harm' – I sat at the kitchen table with Lex and Nicholas while my mum made sandwiches.

'Why don't you three play down here for

while?' she said.

'We're not *playing*, mum,' I said, 'we're having a meeting.'

My mum smiled. 'So have your meeting here, at the table.'

'It's a secret meeting, mum. We can't just have it anywhere.'

'Ooh, sounds very mysterious.'

I rolled my eyes. Nicholas leaned across the table and whispered, 'Why don't we just go back to the clubhouse?'

Lex looked panicked. 'There are no sand-wiches in the clubhouse.'

'Didn't you fill up on mini muffins in the granny clubhouse?'

'No, I only had three.'

My mum plopped a plate full of sand-wiches in the middle of the table and Lex grabbed one.

'Mmm, peanut butter and banana. Yum!'

'You guys eat up,' my mum said, giving my shoulder a squeeze. 'I'll shut the door and take the twins upstairs, and I promise nobody will bother you for at least twenty minutes. Is that long enough for your secret meeting?'

Lex was already tucking into her second sandwich – we weren't going anywhere for a while.

'Yes,' I grumbled, 'that's long enough.'

My mum shut the door and Lex blurted out through a mouthful of sandwich,

'Security guards.'

'What?' I said.

'We could be security guards.'

'That'll never work,' said Nicholas.

'Life guards.'

'We're too young,' I said.

'Sailors,' said Lex.

'What?'

'Or we could run a laundrette.'

'Lex, these are terrible ideas.'

'Oh.'

Lex doesn't usually do a lot of talking, but apparently when she's full of peanut butter and banana she can't shut up.

'Sub-teachers,' she said, taking one more bite.

I stared at her for a minute, then looked at Nicholas.

'Have you got any ideas?'

He thought for a moment and said,

'I think we should make something to sell. We haven't tried that yet.'

'Yeah, but what could we make that people would buy?'

'I made a bunch of fantasy figures once, with that set I got for my birthday.'

'But aren't those sets really expensive?'

'Hm, yeah.'

'Isn't there something else we can make? There must be something.'

After a pause Nicholas smiled.

'I can make fruit pies. Remember when Dad taught me? I made a bunch for you guys, apple ones.'

I squinted at the memory. 'They were a bit doughy.'

'They were *fine*. Besides, I'm sure I can do better this time around. And you guys might actually help, even though you don't know how to bake *at all*.'

I let the last bit go and grabbed one of my parents' recipe books off the counter.

'I think it's a deadly idea. I bet we can make the yummiest pies in the world if we put our minds to it. Look, here! A recipe for pear pies – they look delish!' I drooled over the photo in the recipe book and read the instructions. 'This doesn't sound difficult at all.'

Nicholas turned the book to look.

'Well, we can get the flour and butter and stuff from my house – we've always plenty of stuff for baking – but what about the pears?'

I looked at the fruit bowl on the counter; two bruised apples, a very old mandarin and one last banana that was starting to go brown.

'Uch, nothing here. Lex?'

She shook her head. 'My mum and dad

are doing a no-sugar thing for a few weeks –
no cookies, no muffins ... not even *fruit*. It's
awful.'

'And we've no money,' I said, frowning, 'so
where are we going to get the pears?'

Nicholas gave me a worried look. 'There is
one place, but we're not going to want to go
there.'

I gulped. I knew exactly where he meant,
and he was right. None of us wanted to go
there. But I thought of what Lex's granny had
said about adventure, and I thought about
Nicholas missing out on his masterclass, and
then I clenched my fist and said,

'We *are* going to go there.'

'Are you serious?' said Nicholas.

'I am. The Bubble Street Gang are going to
the empty house.'

There was a pause and Lex looked up from her pile of sandwiches.

'We're *what*?!'

At the back of the empty house, in a garden

that's all wild and overgrown, there's a great big pear tree in one corner. I've only ever seen it from the green behind the back wall (I've never gone into the gardens of the empty house) but some older kids in the street sometimes sneak in and take some pears. It's not stealing – nobody owns the empty house, it's just sitting there empty – and the pears would go to waste otherwise. I've heard they're the juiciest, yummiest pears ever. Perfect for pear pies.

Me and Lex and Nicholas stood at the top of the driveway for a while, but we just couldn't bring ourselves to walk down the drive, slip down the side of the house through the broken gate, and into the back garden. It was just too scary. Being that close to the empty house? Whatever was hiding behind those windows could reach out and grab us. No way.

So, instead, we decided the only way was to go around to the green and climb over the back wall. That was easier said than done; the wall is really high. The older kids climb it, but they're way taller, and they can give each other a leg up.

The only one of us who had a chance of getting up the wall was Lex.

'No way.' She'd gone so pale her lips were white.

'Come on, Lex,' I said, 'we'll be right behind you.'

'No way, no way, no *way*.'

I sighed. 'Well then I'll have to do it, but I don't see how. I can't climb like you.'

'I'll give you a boost.'

'That won't be enough.'

We stood and stared up at the great grey wall for ages.

'I know,' said Nicholas, 'I'll kneel down, like a table, Lex can stand on my back and give you a leg up from there. That'll be enough to get you to the top.'

'What if we squish you?' I said.

'Try not to.'

'Okay, but you can't complain if this hurts, 'cos it's probably going to.'

He was probably going to complain anyway, but I thought it was big of him to volunteer.

Nicholas kneeled down, with his hands sinking into the muddy grass, and Lex stepped onto his back.

'Ow.'

'Sorry.'

Lex laced her fingers and held her hands low so I could put one foot into them. The high wall was scary enough; I tried not to think of where I'd be once I was over.

'On three,' said Lex. 'One, two, *three.*'

Lex is so strong. One lift and I went flying from the ground high enough to grab the top of the wall. But I couldn't lift up and over; my toes started scrabbling on the bricks, until I felt Lex gently grab both my feet and push upwards. She couldn't push me all the way over, but it was like I was standing on her hands. A little jump and I was at the top.

'Ow!' cried Nicholas, down on the ground.

'It's all right,' I said, 'I'm up now.'

I reached down for Lex.

'Do I have to?'

'I'll go in first,' I said, 'but I'm not going in alone.'

I dragged her up the wall and, between us, we managed to get Nicholas up too, until all three of us were perched there.

At the other end of the garden the empty house was big and dark, but the pear tree was much closer.

'I'm going in,' I said.

I slid down the vines that crawled up the inside of the wall. Suddenly feeling brave, I whispered,

'I'll get the pears and throw them up to you. Be ready.'

There were bushes and vines and hanging branches everywhere, it was like walking through a forest. But I finally found the beautiful pear tree. One by one I picked the fruits and cradled them in my jumper. Somewhere, a twig snapped. I spun around, but couldn't see anything. I went back to picking the fruit until I heard the sound of footsteps just ahead. A dark figure was moving through the vines and branches. It got closer and closer. The pears spilled from my jumper. I got ready to run.

Suddenly the figure emerged from a wall of leaves.

'Hello.'

Chapter Eleven

'What's your name?' the boy said.

I froze. I was too terrified to move. He looked like a normal boy, but what if he wasn't? What if he was actually a huge, scary, human-eating monster in disguise?

I turned and ran.

'Wait!' he yelled behind me. 'You forgot your pears!'

I stopped and turned around. He was walking towards me, his arms full of the pears I had dropped.

'My name's Martyn,' he said. 'We just moved here.'

Want to hear something nuts? Martyn is the invisible boy in my class. Martyn Nowak; I remembered his name from the register. Except he's not invisible. He's totally visible.

After I decided the boy in the garden was not a huge, scary, human-eating monster, I called Lex and Nicholas down from the top of the wall. Then Martyn invited us into the kitchen. We walked up the garden and through the back door. It was so weird going into the empty house; I was kind of expecting it to look like a dungeon inside, but the kitchen looked like a very fancy, modern kitchen. There were shiny appliances all over the counter – I don't know what most of them were. We sat down at the table and Martyn opened a cake tin.

'Want some?' he said.

There were lemon and white chocolate squares in the tin, and some triple chocolate cookies too. They were gorgeous.

Lex had had this really nervous expression on her face ever since Martyn appeared, but the cakes and cookies really helped to calm her down.

'We didn't know anyone lived here,' I said, munching on a cookie. 'We thought this house was empty.'

'We only moved in a few weeks ago,' said Martyn. 'Mum says we're going to hire someone to sort out the front and back garden 'cos they're all overgrown. It won't look like an empty house then.'

Martyn was supposed to be in my class – his parents signed him up when they knew they were moving to our town – but at the start of term he got sick, so his parents kept him home. I thought that sounded cool, but it turns out he still has to do schoolwork with textbooks and everything; his mum teaches him.

'You don't look sick now,' Nicholas said. 'Why don't you come to school if you're better?'

'I'm having a good day today,' said Martyn, 'but it might be a bad day tomorrow. When I get sick like this it lasts for ages – sometimes for months – and it's not good for me to be out too much in case I catch a cold or something else. Then I'd be really, *really* sick.'

'That sounds terrible,' I said, 'you must get so bored.'

'Yeah, it does get boring sometimes. I wish I could play out in the street like other kids.

I read a lot of books – spy books and adventure stories and stuff like that – but it'd be nice to be part of an *actual* adventure for once.'

I looked at Lex and Nicholas and I knew they were thinking the same as me. Rule No. 1 of the clubhouse is:

1. The Bubble Street Gang is a secret organisation – NEVER reveal its existence.

But this was a special case.

'I think you just got your wish, Martyn,' I said. 'You're part of *our* actual adventure.'

'What do you mean?'

We told him about the Bubble Street Gang and about our clubhouse. We told him about our club meetings and about building the granny clubhouse. We told him about the costume masterclass and how we set out to make money so Nicholas could go to it. We told him about the Jumble Sale and the Berbel Street Tour and the Virtual Holiday and the Ghost Tour. We told him about Lex falling out of the tree, about the bull in the field and the scary costumes and the money we had to give back. Finally, we told him about the pear pies and why we'd snuck into his back garden.

'We thought the empty house was haunted,' I said. 'That's why I got so scared when you popped out of nowhere.'

'Sorry about that,' said Martyn.

'That's all right. I mean, we were stealing your pears so ...'

'Oh, but you can have all the pears you want.'

'Are you sure?' said Nicholas. 'Won't your parents mind?'

'Not at all, and you know what? You can make the pies here. I'll help you. I'm good at baking.'

'Me too!' said Nicholas. 'My dad taught me and he bakes a cake every other weekend, so he's really good.'

'My dad taught me too! He's a pâtissier – that means pastry chef. He went to a posh cooking school in France, then he worked in a couple of fancy restaurants, and now he's got a tent at the organic market in town every weekend. He sells lots of posh cakes – pain au chocolats, tartes tatin, macarons ...'

We all stared at Martyn as he went on listing fancy cakes we'd never heard of. I thought Nicholas might be jealous – his dad definitely never went to a posh cooking school in France – but he looked too impressed to be jealous.

'Hey,' Martyn said suddenly. 'Dad can help as well! He has the best recipes, and we've got a giant oven for making loads of pies at a time. He might even sell them at the organic market.'

'Do you think he would?' I said.

'Sure!'

I wasn't convinced until we met Martyn's dad. He was really nice and he seemed very happy that Martyn had made some friends. And he really did have the best recipes. He listed a few – we picked the one that sounded the most delicious – and then invited us back the next day to collect the pears and bake the pies.

'And he said he'd sell them for us at the market!' I said to my mum later that evening.

'That sounds wonderful, Cass.'

'And Martyn's really cool and he's not invisible anymore.'

'Oh. Was he invisible before?'

'Sort of. Anyway, is it all right if I go back tomorrow?'

'Of course it is, honey. I'm delighted you've got a new friend.'

I was happy we were so close to making the Bubble Street Gang's first company a success. And then I realised something else; I'd solved the mystery of Invisible Boy.

Some people might say that I didn't; that I'd been wrong all along about there being an invisible boy in my class. But I'm a professional. I go where the evidence leads. And, in the beginning, the evidence led to there being a supernatural kid in my classroom. When the evidence led elsewhere, I followed. Like a true detective. And, like a true detective, my brain was working things out without me even knowing it. Did I sneak into the Nowaks' back garden just to grab some pears? Or, deep down, without even knowing it, did I *know* that the empty house held the answer to the mystery of Invisible Boy?

Yep, that's right. I knew. Deep down, without even knowing I knew, I knew. I marvel at the brilliance of my brain sometimes. It really is something special.

I took out my Top Secret notebook and wrote in big, bold letters:

Operation Invisible Boy: SOLVED

Chapter Twelve

'Be careful up there!'

Martyn's dad was staring up Lex, who was dangling from a branch at the top of the pear tree.

'Oh, don't worry, Mr Nowak, she's fine,' I said. 'She's always hanging off trees and stuff, and she hardly ever falls.'

That didn't seem to set Mr Nowak's mind at rest at all.

'I really wish she'd come down. That's too high.'

'LEX!' I yelled, making Martyn's dad jump. 'Come on down, we've got enough now.'

'You sure?'

'Yeah.'

Lex had been picking the best fruit and chucking it down for me and Nicholas to catch. We caught most of them, but a few slipped past us and hit the ground before we put them in the basket.

'Oh no, no, no, no, no,' Martyn's dad said, plucking out the bruised fruit. 'Only the good ones; the bad pears will ruin the tarts.'

I'd a feeling this baking thing was going to be more complicated than we'd thought. Mr Nowak was really particular; he checked *every single pear* for bruises and holes and bad bits, and wouldn't let us keep any fruit that wasn't perfect.

It took ages, but we finally had a basketful of the most perfect pears anyone's ever seen, so we headed inside.

Martyn wasn't feeling the best, so he couldn't go into the back garden that was full of flowers and plants and things that set off his allergies. He stayed in the kitchen with his mum and helped her make hot chocolate for all of us. It was amazing hot chocolate.

'Belgian,' Martyn's dad said, 'with a hint of hazelnut.'

Wherever it was from, it was gorgeous.

Martyn's mum is so funny. While Mr Nowak set out the weighing scales and bowls and all the ingredients, she drank hot chocolate with us and told us some terrible jokes.

'What do you call an alligator in a vest?'

'I don't know,' I said. 'What do you call an alligator in a vest?'

'An investigator.'

'That's not even funny!'

'Then why are you laughing?'

Another time she made Lex snort hot chocolate out her nose. We laughed at that for about ten minutes.

'All ready,' said Mr Nowak.

Everything was ready now. He was really keen for us to do most of the baking, but he also wanted us to do everything *neatly* and *properly* and to make each pie look *parfait*. I looked up the word 'parfait' later, and I don't understand why he wanted the pies to be parfait.

Definition of parfait:
a creamy, frozen dessert.

Who on earth would want frozen pear pies? Chefs are weird.

Anyway, even though Martyn's dad was running between us correcting everything, the baking was really fun. I felt like a real chef; I was wearing an apron and I'd flour all over my face and butter all over my hands. We rolled out the pastry and cut it into little cups.

'The *same*,' Martyn's dad said, pinching each one. 'They must all be the same in shape

and size. Neat, neat, neat.'

When all the cups were (pretty much) the same shape and size, we filled them with this sticky, almond mixture that was so yummy Lex kept stealing blobs of it out of the bowl.

'What?' said Mr Nowak when he saw the bowl was nearly empty. 'We had enough for six more. Where did it go?'

'That's okay,' I said. 'We can just put a little less in these last few pies.'

'No, no, no, no, they must all be the same!'

I was kind of mad at Lex then because we had to carefully empty each of the pies and refill them, so they all had the same amount of almond mixture. I made sure to keep Lex distracted while the others did the refilling – I didn't want the same thing happening again.

For the final step, we layered thin slices of pear over the mixture, and glazed them with a special syrup so they'd go shiny and golden in the oven.

Martyn's dad looked at the neat lines of mini pear pies like they were the most beautiful thing he'd ever seen.

'Ah,' he sighed, '*parfait.*'

(I still don't get it.)

Then Martyn's mum looked over his shoulder and said, 'You know what you should do, kids? Use the leftover pastry to make shapes for the top of each pie. To make them all individual.'

Mr Nowak looked horrified. Actually horrified, like he'd just seen a huge, grisly, red-eyed monster.

'But they're perfect,' he said, 'they're all

the same!'

'Yes, I know, but don't we want these to stand out as the pies that Martyn and his friends made?'

Mr Nowak went on looking horrified while Martyn and the rest of us started rolling strings of pastry. We thought it was a brilliant idea.

'I'm making a microscope,' I said.

'I'm making a cat's face,' said Martyn.

'A theatre mask,' Nicholas said.

'I think I'll make a frog,' said Lex.

Mr Nowak looked like he might cry.

Chapter Thirteen

The pear pies were a total success! My mum took me to the organic market early, and half of them were already gone.

Martyn's dad had put them right at the front of the display, with a sign in swirly, fancy writing:

All of them sold by the end of the day, and Martyn's mum invited us and our parents to their house to celebrate. They had

homemade lemonade and finger food that was so delicious I can't even describe it. Me, Martyn, Lex and Nicholas filled a plate each and snuck off to the sitting room to play video games.

About half an hour later, Martyn's mum popped her head around the door.

'So,' she said, 'who's the treasurer?'

'Huh?' we all said.

'Who's in charge of the profits? Is it you, Cass?'

She handed me an envelope, then winked and left us alone again. I opened the envelope and gasped. It was full of money.

'Wow! I'd no idea we'd make so much.'

'Is it enough for Nicholas's masterclass?' said Lex.

'Maybe ... but hang on, we have to give Martyn his cut first.'

'No, no,' Martyn said, waving his hands, 'I want it to go to Nicholas's class too. Is it enough?'

I counted out the money on the floor while the others held their breath. Finally, I smiled.

'With eight euro left over!'

'Yay!'

We all cheered and hugged, and I think Nicholas even had a tear in his eye.

'Thanks so much, you guys.'

'You're welcome,' I said, handing him the envelope. 'You should give that to your parents so it doesn't get lost.'

We spent the rest of the evening stuffing ourselves with cakes and snacks, and going through all the deadly boardgames Martyn had in his room.

When I got home I felt all warm and glowy.

We'd done a really good thing – I don't think I've ever seen Nicholas so happy.

I smiled as I got into bed. A new friend, a solo mystery solved and the Bubble Street Gang became (not quite) millionaires. We really were the best secret club ever.

That Sunday there was an exhibition in the arts centre after Nicholas's costume master-class, and my dad took me and Lex to see it (Martyn wasn't well enough to go, so my dad said he'd take lots of photos on his phone that Martyn could look at later).

Definition of exhibition: when an artist makes a bit of art and they want to show it off, they have a special show where people can come and look at the art and give them loads of compliments.

We walked into this big, white room, and all around the walls there were mannequins in weird costumes with people standing next to them, smiling. Nicholas was the youngest person in the masterclass – all of the others were teenagers or adults – and he stood next to his mannequin in the far corner.

I didn't really get Nicholas's costume. It was supposed to be an alien (the sign on the floor said so), but it didn't look much like an actual alien. Actual aliens are short and grey, and they have oval-shaped heads and giant black eyes. I've seen lots of them in comics and on tv shows, so I should know.

Nicholas's alien had a really long head that nearly touched the ground, with insect feelers instead of eyes, and four arms coming out of where its ears should have been. It was hairy too, and had big, flat feet, like a duck.

'What do you think?' Nicholas asked.

He was beaming like he was really proud of himself, so I wasn't sure what to say.

'It's … em … it's different.'

His face fell.

'Yeah, well, I picked an alien so I could just let my imagination run wild. I mean, nobody knows what aliens look like.'

Yes they do, I thought, *they're grey and small with oval-shaped heads.*

I didn't say it out loud though. I just smiled and nodded. Then I heard some terrible, whiny voices behind me.

'What is *that*?'

'Seriously, what is that supposed to be? It's

so rubbish.'

'I feel sorry for the mannequin.'

I turned around, and there stood all three members of the Na-Sa-Ji Club. They were pointing at Nicholas's costume and whispering and snickering. My blood boiled.

Jim Brick's sister had some dance recital in another room in the arts centre – so he had reason to be there – but I bet Nathan and Sasha heard about Nicholas's exhibition and had come especially to make fun of him. They pointed and laughed some more, and Nicholas's face went really, really red.

'Alien?' Nathan said, reading the sign on the floor. 'That's supposed to be an alien? It looks more like Bigfoot wearing clown shoes.'

Sasha and Jim burst out laughing, and

Nicholas just stared at the ground.

I felt like crying, but instead I got really angry.

How would the stupid Na-Sa-Ji Club know what an alien looks like? Nicholas was right – *nobody* knows. And it's not like Nathan or Sasha or Jim could come up with anything so weird and original – not the Na-Sa-Ji Club and their *TINY, TINY minds*! It takes a genius to come up with something that no one else in the world has *ever* come up with. And my friend, Nicholas, is a genius.

'It's brilliant!' I yelled suddenly. 'Seriously, Nicholas, it's the weirdest alien I've ever seen. It's amazing. You're a genius! Woohoo!'

I started clapping really fast and everyone was staring at me. Nicholas went even redder and gave me a look that said,

Why are you clapping? No one else is clapping. Stop clapping.

The Na-Sa-Ji Club were smirking at me, but I kept on clapping. Then I heard Lex join in quietly next to me. Then my dad joined in. Then Nicholas's dad joined in, then Nicholas's mum, then some man I don't know (who might have been the teacher), then some other people from the class joined in, and pretty soon the whole room was clapping and cheering for Nicholas. He was still really red, but he was grinning now.

The Na-Sa-Ji Club disappeared into the crowd, but I didn't care about them anymore. I kept on clapping and grinning at Nicholas, and he kept on grinning back, standing next to his wonderful, weird alien. And then I thought …

Aliens …

Aliens have flying saucers …

I'd noticed a weird circle in the grass in Mrs Leadbetter's front garden the other day …

Flying saucers are circular …

When they land, they must leave a mark …

A *circular* mark …

Oh my god …

Aliens have been landing in Mrs Leadbetter's front garden!

That's what it's like having a brilliant brain. As soon as you solve one mind-boggling mystery, your brain gets *itchy* and goes searching for another.

Aliens have been landing in Mrs Leadbetter's garden. I'm certain of it.

But how to prove it?

Simple. The Bubble Street Gang's next mission is:

Operation Secret Alien Landing

There's no rest for the wicked. Or for genius detectives and their secret gangs.

CLUBHOUSE RULES

1.THE BUBBLE STREET GANG IS A SECRET ORGANISATION — NEVER REVEAL ITS EXISTENCE.

2. NEVER TELL ANYONE OUTSIDE THE BUBBLE STREET GANG ABOUT THE CLUBHOUSE.

3.THE BUBBLE STREET GANG SWEARS TO SEARCH OUT ADVENTURE, SOLVE MYSTERIES, FIGHT FOR JUSTICE AND BE GOOD ~~ENTERPRINEERS~~ ~~ENTREPENORS~~ BUSINESSPEOPLE.

4.NO FRUIT, BROWN BREAD OR OTHER HEALTHY FOOD IS TO BE CONSUMED IN THE CLUBHOUSE.

5.THE CLUBHOUSE LIBRARY IS FOR EXCITING, DANGEROUS, DETECTIVE OR FUNNY BOOKS ONLY. NO SCHOOLBOOKS.

6.MEMBERS WILL TAKE TURNS TO REFILL THE SNACK JARS.

7.ALWAYS CLOSE THE CLUBHOUSE DOOR WHEN YOU ARE LAST OUT.

8.SECRET DOCUMENTS MUST BE LOCKED AWAY IN THE HARRY POTTER BOOK-SAFE DURING THE NIGHT.

9.IF YOU'RE EATING SOMETHING CRUMBLY YOU MUST USE A PLATE. NO-ONE WANTS MICE IN THE CLUBHOUSE.

10.ANY MEMBER CAN DEMAND HELP FROM OTHER MEMBERS IN MATTERS OF LIFE OR DEATH (OR IF IT'S JUST REALLY, REALLY IMPORTANT).

ANYONE WHO BREAKS ANY OF THE RULES OF THE CLUBHOUSE MUST BE PUNISHED.

Read an extract from the first book
about Cass and the Bubble Street Gang –

The Clubhouse Mystery

Chapter One

Do you want to know a secret? Well, I can't tell you. I absolutely cannot tell you. It's the biggest, most exciting secret I've had in weeks, maybe even months. I mean, I could tell you, but then I'd have to kill you. So, you see, I absolutely cannot tell you ...

All right, how about I tell you and you promise not to tell anybody else? Not even your best friend. Not even your pet. Not even your pet even if your pet is also your best friend. Cross your heart and hope to die? Okay then, you've twisted my arm.

We've built a fort. A secret fort. A *clubhouse*.

I probably should have mentioned first that I'm in a secret club. Well, here goes, the entire secret: I'm in a secret club and now we've got a secret clubhouse.

The idea came (as so many of my ideas do) from the desperate need to get out of the house and away from the annoying baby twins. It was Saturday morning and I had built an epic fort in the sitting room. It involved one sofa, one mop, two armchairs, two dining chairs, the pouffy/footstool thing that my mum likes, and five (that's right, FIVE) blankets. It was nearly tall enough to stand up in, there was a window (made using a bunch of clothes pegs off the washing line) through which I could watch TV, and the whole thing was protected by an invisible force field.

Unfortunately, although the force field was effective in keeping out aliens, monsters and Bigfoot, it was apparently no match for the annoying baby twins. They demolished the entire fort in about ten seconds flat.

'Daaad!' I yelled up the stairs. 'The twins wrecked my fort.'

'Did they?' he called back. 'Well, don't worry, honey, you can build it again.'

That didn't help at all.

'Muuum!' I yelled. 'The twins wrecked my fort.'

'They just want to play with you, Cass,' she called back. 'Why don't you pick something you can all play together?'

Play with the *annoying baby twins*? That's a ridiculous suggestion. Before they were born I might have thought it was a great idea. I'd had the house to myself for eight whole years – I was the queen of the castle, I ruled the roost – but when my parents told me I had two brothers or sisters on the way I was really excited. Two more kids, as funny and clever as me, to share adventures with and laugh at all my hilarious jokes? Bring it on.

But instead of two brilliant siblings my parents came home with Pippi and Ade; a pair of bulldozers in babygros. Pippi will chew anything she can get her grubby hands on. She puts EVERYTHING in her mouth. Ade, on the other hand, won't eat anything. Food goes in his hair or up his nose or on the floor or all over my dad's shirt. Come to think of it, I'm not sure I've ever seen any food go into Ade's mouth. Shouldn't he be hungry by now? Ugh, babies are weird.